Grease Stains, Kismet and Maternal Wisdom

Mel
Bosworth

(BrownpaperpublishinG)

First Printing

ISBN: 978-1-45385-925-4

Published By Brown Paper Publishing

www.brownpaperpub.wordpress.com
www.eddiesocko.blogspot.com

Printed in the United States of America

For Ginny

Grease Stains,
Kismet and
Maternal Wisdom

When I awoke Monday morning to drive to Hudson to meet Samantha, I didn't know that the uncle she and her mother were staying with for the week had suffered an accident during the night. Moments after leaving my house, my truck revving toward the center of town, I got the call.

The day was vivid and clear, warm. My face was clean, my beard trimmed, and my bag packed. I was dressed in corduroys, a long sleeved shirt and vest even though I could've gotten away with shorts and a T-shirt. I was already on my tenth cigarette.

'Hello?'

'David? It's Samantha. I have to tell you something.'

'Go.'

'You're not going to believe this.'

'What?'

'Last night my uncle fell in the hallway and broke his leg.'

'No fucking way.'

'We had ambulances and paramedics here at four in the morning. He's in the hospital now in Benton.'

'Is he alright?'

'Well, he broke his leg. But he's doing okay.'

'Good god.'

Then something occurred to me: maybe she was telling me this because she didn't want me to come. She'd decided during the night that she didn't like me, didn't trust me, didn't want to see my mug. This whole uncle thing was a crock. Samantha was a chicken shit. So I asked

'Samantha?'

'Yes?'

'Are you a chicken shit?'

'No. I'm more of a bat shit. Bat shit loony, that is.'

No. That didn't happen. Take two.

'Samantha?'

'Yes?'

'Do you still want me to come?'

There was a miniscule pause, nothing to fret over, but I heard it.

'Yes, of course I still want you to come. So, you should be here…?'

'Around twelve thirty-ish. I'll call when I get to Hudson. But I think I can find my way to you.'

'I can't believe my uncle broke his leg.'

'I can't believe it either. What was he doing?' I asked, still driving, still moving in the direction of Hudson, my tires spinning past the town common and the clay pulling ring that had been set up for the annual Fair that coming weekend where, amidst a pungent concoction of fried dough, cotton candy and manure, the oxen would snort and jerk, the rednecks would scream, the whips would crack, and the cursing would share the air with projectile spit.

Samantha sighed. She sounded lovely. An ephemeral thought of her naked flashed behind my eyes.

'He was rummaging around under a rug looking for some M&Ms he'd dropped.'

'Why was he eating M&Ms at four in the morning?'

'I don't know.'

'That's weird.'

'Yes it is. *So weird*, David, that it's not even true. Can we stick to the facts, please?'

'Maybe. But I like this story. It's funny.'

'The real story is funny too.'

'Fine. You're right. Absolutely right. I'm sorry.'

'I know I'm right. I'm always right. My name is Samantha and I'm always right.'

'Typical woman.'

'You're still off track.'

'Oh, am I?'

'Knock it off.'

She was getting heated now. I could feel it coming through my cell phone like hot air from a blow dryer.

'Fine,' I said. 'I'll be there soon. Do you still want to go to the city?'

'Yes. We can still do whatever. My mother's going to visit my uncle at the hospital sometime this afternoon, and we can still do whatever we want.'

'Can I stick my tongue up your ass in the backseat of my truck?'

'No. That's *Friday* night, David. And it's not the backseat of your truck but the floor of the studio at the house in Hudson. Your knees get a little rug burned. Don't you remember?'

'Oh, yeah. You're right.'

'Like I said, my name is Samantha and I'm always right.'

'Typical woman.'

'Hey, asshole—'

I hung up on her and lit another cigarette, number eleven. I steered the truck out of town, through Cold Creek and then onto the Massachusetts Turnpike.

I've forgotten my sunglasses, but no worries, I thought. *I'm traveling east at the moment and if all goes well, I won't be driving back west tonight all by myself and the sun won't be in my eyes. Hotels,* I had been thinking, as far back as the week before. *Hotels.*

The Pike was busy but moving, bright but not blurring. Cranking my 'Red Sox Rock' mix that I'd made back in August for a game, I sang loudly, and at one point I worried that I might lose my voice by the time I got there, so I decided to sing at a lower decibel.

I drove, I smoked, I screamed occasionally. Passing through Hopkinton, the town in which the Boston Marathon begins, I decided that now might be a good time to call my friend Mark, just for a little security.

'What?'

'Hey, which exit do I take to get to Hudson? It's been a while.'

'Exit 21. Then get on 20 North. It's like the first exit after that, I think.'

'Right, right. It's all coming back to me now. Do you know where Main Street is?'

'Do you remember how to get to my old place on Barker Street?'

'I think so.'

'Main Street runs perpendicular to Barker.'

Great, I thought. *Fucking geometry. Perpendicular. Is that the 'T'? I think it's the 'T.' I know parallel is side by side and so that must mean that perpendicular is the 'T.'*

'Right,' I said, stupidly. Mark was growing impatient.

'Anything else?'

'Yeah.'

'What?'

'What are you doing?'

'I'm at work, what the fuck do you think I'm doing?'

'Right. What are you doing later?'

'I don't know. Not much, probably.'

'Do you and Janice want to hang out later?'

'I doubt it. I'm tired.'

'Right, right.'

'Go find your girlfriend. Call me if you get fucked up in Hudson.'

'I will.'

'I know you will.'

I laughed a sick little laugh and then I brought

my full attention back to the road. Exit 21 approached to my right. I was close now. Very close. I was going to stop at Burger King on the corner of Moon Street in Hudson to change my shirt and make myself look as pretty as a goofy looking fuck like me could look. These actions too were a part of my master plan that ended in a hotel room somewhere with Samantha, my pen pal from the west coast who I'd met only once and barely knew. I was optimistic, but not cocky. I could do humble well. And jealous. And crazy.

Finally, things began to look familiar. I found my way around some turns and chutes and over a bridge and then I spotted Burger King. I parked in back next to a dumpster. I was giddy, nervous, and, unbeknownst, even to me, I'd entered into an alternate universe, a *parallel* universe, blanketed in some kind of silly spell that wouldn't break until the following Monday.

I grabbed my backpack and walked stiff legged into the King. It was the lunch hour and it was busy. I went into the bathroom and into the single stall. I relieved myself and then I took off my shirt. It was wet because I'd been sweating nervous sweat and I put on a fresh shirt, a button shirt, and someone came into the bathroom and started making a hell of a racket.

There was heavy breathing and then big splashes of water and lots of coughing. I stuffed my dirty damp shirt into my backpack and tucked myself in and came out of the stall. One of the employees, a tall black man wearing a blue Burger King shirt, had come to piss and wash his hands. I smiled and moved to the sink. He left and I was alone once more. I looked in the mirror.

My hair was a little windblown so I ran my hands over it. *Better.* My eyes were a little bloodshot but there was nothing I could do about that. I was wired. I'd been wired for a while. The fifteen cigarettes probably hadn't helped.

But all in all, I thought, *I look about as good as I can get. I wonder what Samantha will be wearing. A bikini might be nice. We're in the midst of late Indian summer so it's certainly warm enough for it. Will we chat or will we go right for the sex? Hard to say…but I do know that things will be decided in the first 2.2 seconds of meeting. In those 2.2 seconds she'll know if I'm to be the father of her children. Lots of pressure, to be sure, but I've been pretty solid for a while. Calm. Cool. Collected. Idiotic. Hopeful.*

I'd stopped my truck screaming some time ago, and now the screaming had become entirely internalized yet surprisingly controlled, or at least dulled, like a gaping shriek muffled beneath a huge pillow. I was both shrieker *and* pillow holder. I washed my hands and left the King. *Game on.*

I climbed back into my truck and called my mother.

'Hey, I'm in Hudson.'

'How was traffic?'

'Not bad at all. What are you doing?'

'Sitting out on the deck. What a gorgeous day. So, do you know where you're going?'

'I think so. I have to call Mark.'

'That's a good idea.'

'Yeah. Well, I should call him and then I have to call Samantha and try not to get lost.'

'Drop a line sometime to let us know when you're coming home.'

'I will. But I'm thinking it'll be sometime tomorrow morning. They have to go visit her uncle who broke his leg last night.'

'Let me guess—searching for M&Ms?'

'You're a fucking psychic, Mom.'

'I knew you were going to say that.'

'Of course you did. Well, so long. I'll give you a call when I hit the road.'

'Sounds good. Have a good time.'

'I will. I love you.'

'I love you too.'

I smiled. I lit another cigarette and called Mark.

'Hey, I'm in Hudson.'

'Good for you.'

'How the fuck do I get to Main Street? I'm at the Burger King near your old place.'

'Okay…'

I could tell that Mark knew more this time. He wasn't going to spring 'perpendicular' on me again. I hated that shit.

'You know the street you were just on? Moon?'

'Why are you calling me 'Moon'?'

'No, not *you*, you fuckshow. The street, *Moon Street*.'

'Yeah.'

Mark hadn't appreciated my joke.

'Well, get back on that and follow it to the end. You'll run right into Main Street.'

'I don't suppose you know Chess Street?'

'Not a fucking clue, dude.'

'Right. Well, if I can find Main I'm sure I can find Chess.'

'I'm sure you can.'

There was a pause. I was getting nervous again. I was sure I was only minutes away from Samantha. I could smell her. I heard Mark shift. I imagined him lying on a waterbed.

'Anything else?' he asked.

'Yeah. What are you doing tonight?'

'I don't think I can hang out, dude. Go find your girlfriend.'

'I will. Thank you.'

'Yup. Give me a call if you need anything.'

'I will.'

'I know you will.'

I hung up. I lit another cigarette. I called Samantha.

'Hello?'

'I'm in Hudson!' I sang. *I'm a dork too. Idiot and dork.*

'Yay!' Samantha cheered. Or at least I thought she cheered. She could have been booing and I wouldn't have known the difference.

'I should be there in a few minutes,' I said.

'I'll be waiting outside for you.'

'What are you going to be wearing?'

Say bikini. Say bikini.

'A bikini.'

Yes!

'Really?'

'No. David, can we get back to the real story?'

'I'm on my way.'

'Call if you get lost.'

'I will,' I said, thinking, *You have no idea where I'm going either. You've never been to Massachusetts before. But we're close. Very close.*

I hung up. I lit another cigarette. I checked my supply of green tic tacs. *Plenty. Don't smoke any more cigarettes*, I thought. Then, *Do I hug her when I find her? Of course. Kiss? On the cheek, you dumbass. Right. On the cheek. This is crazy. You met this girl three months ago three thousand miles away at three in the morning and you were buck naked. Yes, yes, but it makes total sense. This is normal. This is what people do.*

I started my truck and then pulled out onto Moon Street. I crawled through the center of Hudson. People were everywhere. The sidewalks were warm. The road was warm. I could see the end of the street.

Main Street! Yes! Take a left. How did I know to take a left? Did Samantha tell me that? No! She told me something about...fuck...something she told me led me to take a left, just like something I did three months ago told her to come next door at three in the morning. The spell is over us all, the spell is over us all, relentless.

I took the left. I kept my eyes open.

Chess. Fucking Chess. I can see Chess.

I took a right onto Chess. Now I was looking for Ledgewood.

So close oh my god so close. There it is!

I drove past it. I spun around and came back. I turned onto Ledgewood, feeling like a criminal.

Rows of pine trees cast long shadows across the pavement.

What am I looking for? A fork? Some kind of fork that leads to a house? Yes, that's right. I'm looking for Samantha. In a bikini. No. Not a bikini. It doesn't matter now.

I popped a couple of tic tacs.

Or maybe I did before. Don't remember. Where is this woman?

I turned into a half circle driveway. But I was wrong, I knew I was wrong. I came back out onto the narrow hill that was Ledgewood and then I saw her. Samantha was walking down the next driveway. The sun was at her back, her face dark.

It's her it's her it's her! Are my hands shaking? What have I gotten myself into? What is this?

Instinctively, I thrust my hand out the window.

Hello! It's me! You don't know me! I don't know you! But you're here from Washington and now we're together!

She wore a long tight skirt and a striped green tank top.

Oh...my...fucking...God.

She had straight dark hair that danced around her shoulders. She was smiling and waving and coming toward me. But I was so nervous I drove right past her. My window was down and I spoke in gibberish.

'Shnergle flergle!'

Luckily, she seemed to speak the same language.

'Shnergle!' she exclaimed.

I parked beneath a towering blue spruce and steadied myself as quickly as possible. Then I got out, fighting an overwhelming urge to slide tackle her into a shrub. I could see green moss and a big old house and trees and rocks and this narrow driveway and this gorgeous woman coming toward me, and who am I and what am I doing and what is this and the gibberish intensified, 'Blip-de-dooo!'

'Chomp-di-flip!'

And she was fucking stunning and I felt so ugly nasty such a complete fuck no I didn't, I felt amazing and excited and we were getting closer and closer and our arms opened and then we were embracing and her face was so bright brighter than the sun and she was tight so tight she could kick my ass and did I kiss her cheek I think I did and did she kiss mine I think she did and my heart was racing and I was there and she was there and what the fuck was she doing there and what the fuck was I doing there but it was good it was great this was just the beginning and my plan what plan I had no idea wiped away I couldn't think straight I was embracing this sparkling woman and we parted and I was unsteady and she opened her mouth and she said

'You're here.'

'You're here.'

'I can't believe you're here.'

'I can't believe you're here.'

Her skin was warm like the sidewalks, like the street, covered in the sun and there were those fucking hazel eyes that had been haunting me in my dreams for the past three months, there they were, right in front of me. She spoke again.

'David?'

'Samantha?'

I was completely in love with her.

'How was the drive?'

'Drive? I think I'm flying.'

'Are you nuts?'

'Absolutely.'

'Good. Because I'm nuts too.'

'Really?'

'Absolutely.'

Samantha stepped aside and offered a grand sweeping gesture toward the house. My eyes bugged out of my head.

'Shall we go inside?'

'Indeed.'

'I'll give you the tour.'

I followed her up the cracked cement steps toward the house. I was smiling. I wasn't screaming anymore. I was singing, I was dancing, I was floating, I was electric, I was enraptured. I'd finally found my girlfriend. And she was *nothing* like I remembered. She was so much more.

And I knew, in the back of my mind, that underneath her clothes was a black bikini, or at least a pair of black panties with a red gun printed on the crotch.

one **TWO** three four five six

The house was an old, white, two-story colonial with a slate roof and lots of windows. Inside, it was pleasantly musty and cool. I followed Samantha through the foyer. My shaking had increased so dramatically that I had turned to stone, albeit moveable stone. My eyes were wide brown and darting and any second I expected someone to jump out and club me over the head.

'Ouch!'

'You don't belong here!'

'Why did you hit me with that club?'

'I didn't hit you with any club. This is just your imagination.'

'Well, *good.*'

I tried not to stare at Samantha. This was the first time I'd seen her with sober eyes. The same was true for her. Our chance meeting three months earlier in Washington had been oddly powerful, and enough to keep our 3000 mile string drawn tight. Her arms were long and slender. She moved gracefully.

'This is my uncle's house,' she said. 'When my mother asked if I wanted to come here to visit for a week, I knew I had to.'

Samantha was young and poor like me. When a friend of mine had offered to buy me a roundtrip ticket to visit him in Washington, I took it. Samantha was his neighbor then. A week after I had gone, she moved back to California to live with her mother. That's when the letters began.

The house was huge and tall and wide, filled with creaking stairs and corners. Samantha explained that throw rugs were placed strategically over the hardwood to hide stains. The kitchen was floored with dull white tile. I moved toward the windows by the sink and looked outside. My truck was at the bottom of the driveway.

'I like this place,' I said. *It reminds me of my house.*

'I like it too. It's so old, so big.'

We looked at each other and laughed.

'Yeah.'

'Yeah.'

'Do you want some tea?' she asked.

'I would love some tea.'

'Let me put the kettle on, dear.'

'I'm so in love with you. Isn't that retarded?'

Samantha put a finger to her lips, her face thoughtful. Her nails were long and glossy, pretty, pink. Then she said, 'No…it's not *that* retarded. I can think of more retarded things.'

'I suppose you're right.'

'You know how it goes.'

'Yes, I do.'

I leaned against the counter, unsure of what to do with my hands. I wanted to eat them. I noticed then that the kitchen was dressed in unique wallpaper in which acts of bestiality were depicted between men and goats. *Very Greek*, I thought to myself. Samantha poured the steaming brew into two small cups that had little handles for little fingers.

'Thank you.'

I love you. Stop thinking that. I can't help it.

We sipped our tea quietly. Then a car moved up the driveway.

'My mother's back.'

Samantha's mother was a short round woman with a big smile. We shook hands.

'Hello, David.'

'Hello.'

'Do you like the wallpaper?'

My eyes moved over the prints again, men on goats.

'I do. I like it very much. Very…colloquial.'

'Yes,' she said. 'My brother is a very colloquial man. He's 87, you know?'

'Amazing…This house is so big.'

I was growing stupider by the second.

'Yes…Have you seen the studio? I think you and my daughter are going to have clumsy, drunken, unprotected sex in there sometime this week.'

Samantha winked at me. I stiffened.

'Yes, the studio is quiet lovely,' I said. 'Much like you.'

Her mother blushed, waving off my comment.

'Oh, you Massachusetts boys.'

I looked to Samantha and returned the wink. We were partners in crime. She slapped the teacup from my hand. It landed upright in the sink without breaking.

'What did you do that for?' I asked.

'We have to get this story rolling, fuckshow. Can we get to Cambridge already? Get to the good stuff.'

'But this *is* the good stuff,' I pointed out. 'Men on goats.'

'I know…but get to the part where I spill pizza grease on my shirt, or better, when I ask you if you've ever jerked off thinking about me.'

'But that's like part four, or something. That's a long ways away. I still have to do Harvard Square and the tea place and when we rub heads in line.'

'You're too sappy. Get on with it already.'

Her mother was looking at us, quizzically. Deep creases flexed across her forehead. She didn't know that we were visitors from a parallel universe.

'Why don't I let you two kids get going? There's only so much daylight left and I know you've got a lot of catching up to do.'

'You're right, Mom. David, let's go. Wait, I have to change out of this sexy skirt and put on some jeans.'

'Oh yeah?'

'Oh yeah.'

Samantha slipped out of the room and up a flight or two of stairs. I smiled at her mother and she smiled back. Then she moved close to me. She took my hand and slowly massaged my thumb. Her hands were affectionate, soft.

'You're a dirty boy, aren't you?' she asked.

'I don't know.'

She moved closer. I could smell chocolate milk

on her breath. She closed her eyes and I closed mine and we kissed.

'I always hit on my daughter's boyfriends,' she explained.

'I see.'

Then she put on her innocent, doe eyed face.

'You're not going to tell on me?' she pouted.

'No, of course not.'

'Good.'

She sighed and patted my hand. Then she let go. She moved to the studio.

'And don't forget,' she called through the doorway. 'Friday night, leaves and twigs.'

What does that mean? I wondered. *Are all mothers psychics?*

'Yes we are.'

I jumped.

Where is Samantha? I wondered. This was all getting very strange.

'Ready?'

I turned, and Samantha was standing in front of me. She had put on jeans.

'I'm ready.'

I moved close to her ear.

'Can I tell you something?'

'What?'

'Your mother—'

Then, from the other room, 'What the fuck did I just tell you, David?'

I shook my head.

'Let's just go.'

'Good.'

We said our goodbyes to her mother, went outside into the early afternoon sun, and drove toward the center of Hudson. Samantha smiled next to me. My cell phone rang. It was my old friend Gus from Washington.

'It's Gus,' I said. 'Do you want to talk to Gus?'

'Okay…Hello?'

'Hello? Who's this?'

'This is Samantha, your old neighbor.'

There was a long pause and then I heard him say, 'Ohhh! Right! Samantha! You must be with David.'

'Yes, I'm sitting next to him. We're going to Boston.'

'That's fantastic. How do you like Massachusetts?'

'It's great. My uncle broke his leg.'

'M&Ms?'

'Isn't that joke getting a little old?'

'Right. Anyway, can I talk to David for a minute?'

'Sure. It was nice to talk to you, Gus. Tell Darlene that I said 'Hello.''

'I sure will. You have a good time, and don't ever do shots with that bearded fuck sitting next to you.'

'What do you mean?'

'Oh, you'll find out. But you were jacked up on coke and he was a liter deep in whiskey when you guys met, so I'm sure it can't be any crazier than that. But you never know.'

'Okay…Here's David.'

Samantha handed me the phone then stuck her head out the window. The breeze rippled her hair like black satin. I pressed the phone tightly to my ear and navigated through the hustle and bustle of Hudson central.

'What? What do you want?'

I was Mark now. I imagined myself on a waterbed.

'Hey, buddy. Got a little friend with you today?'

'Yes, I do.'

'Are you gonna eat her pussy?'

'I thought we'd go to Harvard Square this afternoon.'

'Why don't you answer my question? Are you gonna eat her pussy?'

'Thanks, Gus. I gotta go. I hate being that guy.'

'What guy? The guy who doesn't answer my questions?'

'Alright, then. You have a good afternoon.'

'Fuck you, you bastard. Answer my fucking ques—'

I hung up on Gus and then put the phone in the cup holder between the seats. I tapped Samantha on the leg and she pulled her head back into the truck.

'Gus is such a goofball,' I said.

'He's nice.'

'Yes, he's nice.'

'Darlene's nice too.'

'Yes, she is.'

And she has huge fake tits, I thought to myself, grinning.

We chatted and sputtered and rid ourselves of some nervous energy as we searched out Cambridge and Central Square. I parked behind Mark's old apartment building, four stories of red brick that stood in front of a baseball field with basketball courts to the right. I'd brought two balls: a man's and a woman's.

'Do you want to play a quick game of egg?' I asked.

'What's egg?'

'It's like horse only it's egg.'

'Oh…Yeah, let's play.'

We walked over to the courts. A heavily bearded

black man was sitting on the bleachers. He rapped
his cane on the metal as we moved by.

'White people!' he yelped.

We stopped.

'Yes?' I asked.

He wore mirrored sunglasses. His beard was gray
and gnarled. Smiling broadly, wisely, he said,

'You can't play basketball right now.'

'Why not?' asked Samantha.

'You have so many other important things to get
to, this could take forever.'

'But this is important too,' I said. 'We're testing
out our *chemistry*.'

He leaned back and looked to the sky. Then he
roared, 'Bullshit! Get on with it! Like the young
woman said before, get to the fucking pizza place,
or better, the sushi bar!'

'But what about The Re-poo-blick?' I asked. 'Or
the Cantab Lounge?'

He rapped his cane again and we both jumped. I
dropped the basketball and it rolled out of sight.

'Fuck that shit!' he said. 'All foreplay! Stop
teasing me with this crap! Get to the center of this
thing and stop tap dancing around the edges! You
bunch of cowards!'

I looked at Samantha, frowning.

'What do you think?' I asked.

'We *could* go to the pizza place.'

'But I'm not sure anything *big* happens there.'

'*Something* must happen there.'

'Yeah, you spill grease on your shirt and I love you.'

'Well…where do *you* want to go? You're the one telling this story.'

I stuck my fingers into my ears and thought for a moment.

Fuck. How to swing this? I could write it really fast without punctuation like a free write. That way it'll still be significant and nothing, nothing big anyway, will be omitted. This I can do.

'Free write?' I asked, tentatively.

Samantha rolled her eyes, two hazel marbles. The fictitious bearded black man applauded and whistled.

'Whatever,' she said. '*Your* story. What the fuck do I know? I'm only *in* it.'

'Shut up. Are you ready?'

'I guess.'

'Okay. Hang on. And keep your eyes moving.'

'Yes, my love.'

The sun was strong and high in the early afternoon and we were in Cambridge and we were at the basketball courts and we played egg and Samantha was good and she slaughtered me with ease and I grumbled and grunted and we played a best of three and she had a magnificent mid-range game and her feet were fast and she was strong and could get to wherever she wanted to get on the court nine free throws in a row we played but not too hard and we didn't get sweaty and then we left the courts and walked the shady sidewalk up toward Central Square and I asked Are you hungry and she said Yes and I asked Do you want real food or junk food and we had a discussion on the difference and something about falafels was mentioned and then she said pizza and she was adorable just like she was in Seattle when the sun was coming up and I was in her bed and so we walked the sidewalks and we smoked and she told me that I'm tall and then we were in Central Square and we crossed over the paths of buses and the streets were warm and people were out and about wicked smart kids and the bums and I could smell food wherever we went and so we took a right and went down the street and finally we came upon a pizza place and it was warm inside and greasy and smelly and so we got pizza and soda and Samantha rumbled about getting a beer and I thought that that might be a good idea but not right now I'm still so dehydrated and wired and we

sat down and ate our pizza and I looked in and she
looked out and I asked how the view was and she
said she could see the street and I was looking at
Gino the pizza guy and I burned my mouth but
played it cool Samantha wanted another slice and
so she got one and while she was gone I smiled
and shook my head and wondered what the fuck
was going on here she came back with more pizza
and we ate and we talked and she spilled pizza
grease on her shirt and then we left the pizza place
and headed back toward the T and I called Mark
and asked Inbound or Outbound for Harvard
Square and he told me Outbound and I said
Thanks Mark and then we got to the T and we
went down the stairs and the tunnel echoed and
we got through the turnstiles and then we waited
for the train and the train came and we got on and
it rattled and squealed into Harvard Square and we
got off and climbed up to the street more people
than Central Square and fuck I just realized I
missed a bunch of shit The Cantab and The
Republic and drinks and darts and Samantha won
and every time she went to pull her darts from the
board I was staring at her ass she must have
known we played scratch-tickets at The Cantab but
that was before The Republic and we won some
money but left about even and Jameson Whiskey

and beer and Guinness and I wanted to kiss her then but it was early don't fuck this up now but flirt and be merry and then we climbed the stairs to the street in Harvard Square and we went to buy cameras and we took silly pictures of each other and I was pretty buzzed still and I was getting tired and she suggested we go get some coffee and tea and so we went to the coffee/tea place and we waited in line and it was hot inside and we rubbed heads for a moment and I wanted to kiss her neck but I didn't and we got our coffee tea waters too and we went outside and sat in the grass and the sun was going down and the sky was dark blue and purple and Samantha must have been growing cold but she said no she's fine and she called her mother and they talked for a moment and we smoked cigarettes and then I called Mark and asked him where's a good sushi bar and he told me to get back on Massachusetts Avenue and go past the big dolphin and it's right there and I said Thanks and then I lay down in the grass and I wanted to pull her on top of me a human blanket steamroller and we motivated and moved and we stopped at a 7-11 so I could get cigarettes and Samantha crouched with some bums that talked to her about planes and I came out and we gave them cigarettes and then we moved off we found the sushi place easily and it was getting dark it was late it was 8 o'clock maybe and we went inside and it was pretty empty and we sat at the bar and we chatted and ordered food and they didn't have tempura dammit and so we ordered some kind of salty pea pod things that Samantha loved and she taught me how to eat them by pulling out the peas with my teeth she was so nice and we got sake and sushi and Miso soup and it was yummy and we ate and some tourist sat next to us not knowing that we too were tourists and he asked us what we were eating and we looked at him blankly and Samantha said food and he seemed satisfied with that and we drank to us we drank to ourselves this was a celebration and then we were done we said thank you to the nice people and we went outside to have a smoke and we sat on the steps and then I said this is what I'm thinking I'm thinking I'm good enough to drive and I'm thinking I was going to get a room somewhere and then we could do whatever and she said that's fine I'm up for whatever I'll go with you that's fine and I was so fucking happy then that she wasn't going to go back to Hudson and I wasn't going to be alone and I didn't know if we were going to sleep together or what was going to happen but I just knew that she was going to stay with me and that was amazing we're not crazy we got back on the sidewalk and it was dark but still warm the trains kept the sidewalks warm just like the subways in New York the snow never builds up on the sidewalks they are so hot there and then then then she reached over and took my hand and I was so touched so moved so filled that I wanted to drop I wanted to absorb her through osmosis and we walked back toward the T in Harvard Square and we found our way down and it was big and open underneath like a dome and she said it reminded her of New York City even though she'd never been there but it should because it is like New York City only smaller and cleaner and we went through the turnstiles again and we heard music and then we saw the music it was a black dude singing in front of speakers and he wore a Yankee jersey a Philadelphia jersey and he was really good and Samantha wanted to give him some money and I did too and so I handed her a couple of singles and she went over and I watched her go over and she was my girlfriend now whether she liked it or not and the music got louder as she came back over to me because the singing man loved her as much as I did and then the train came and we got on and it was emptier this time and we sat down and we waved to the singing man and he waved back and I wanted to pull her over onto my lap and we got back to Central Square and we climbed up to the street and it was nighttime and we went down Western Avenue and we stopped and bought PowerAde drinks and then she had to pee and so she went into this sketchy little bar and I heard people scream as I waited outside and then a black woman came out laughing and I laughed too but I wasn't sure why and she told me that Samantha tried to go into the men's room better not do that she said and I laughed and Samantha came out and we laughed about it and then we went back to the parking lot behind Mark's old place and we were a little tired a little groggy and so we played basketball again but this time we played one on one hardcore and she was so fucking good and there was a crowd this time cheering her on because they loved her too just like those guys later in the week that wanted to kidnap her and kill me and I was sweating like a fuck and she was so fast and tight with that little mid-range game and I was tired and so I turned on the faucet and let it rain Three Three Three Stop it Oh My God Three Three Three And I had told her that I was the master of the Three-bomb and she didn't believe me but she could still kill me one on one I suck off the dribble and then we finished and we were

happy and full and it was time to call Mark and
figure out what's next and so I did after I ran off
and peed in an alley I called Mark and he told me
to go to the Howard Johnson on the left before
the bridge but it turned out to be the Radisson
which was fine and we found out that it was 150
bucks for a night Good God but Samantha rocked
she threw 50 down because she could sense that I
was running low and we got room 700 and we
were close to the Charles River and Boston
University and I was wearing my black fleece now
and it was covered in cat hair and I was wearing
my Red Sox hat and we were both kind of dirty
and we found the room and Samantha tried the
key card and it didn't work right away and we're
smart people we can do this and finally she got it
to work because she was a genius and I was a
fucking moron and we went inside and kicked off
our shoes and we had two beds in the room and I
sat on one and she sat on the other and we asked
well what do we do now and I had definite ideas
but I still wasn't sure where she was at but I could
imagine and she looked at me funny but not funny
ha ha she looked at me like she wanted me to kiss
her or she wanted to kiss me and we hadn't kissed
yet today and I didn't know I had been thinking
about everything so much and we touched feet

socked feet and she was still looking at me like that and her eyes were so fucking pretty she was so fucking pretty and sweet and funny and sexy and so I moved over to her bed and we hugged and kissed and we hugged and smooched and we smooched and smooched and I had a raging hard-on and I wanted to tear her clothes off and maybe she asked me who are you and I asked who are you and I decided that I must take a shower I was so grimy and gross and I'd been sweating all fucking day and so I jumped up and went to the bathroom and I left the door open intentionally I wanted her to come in and take a shower with me but she didn't which was fine because in a few days I was going to watch her take a bath I came out of the bathroom and she was on the bed with her eyes closed my God she must have been so tired so far away from home so far from anything that she knew she didn't even know me but she was here and she trusted me and I loved that because I trusted her too and I climbed into my jeans and then I climbed next to her and she was warm and quiet and soft like a pillow and we started smooching again and then she was sitting in my lap and I asked her to take her clothes off and so she took her shirt off and wait—

Mel Bosworth

Room 700 at the Radisson in Cambridge was a smoking room with two beds. We would only use one of the beds and we wouldn't even smoke that much, even though there were several ashtrays around the room and even one in the bathroom.

Outside, it was dark and cool. The black waters of the Charles River pushed easily alongside the slow road. Samantha was topless and sitting on my lap.

'Who *are* you?'

'I'm *me*. Who are *you*?'

We could have played this game for hours, and at that moment, it felt like we had hours, and maybe we did in a sense, but the heavy pull of the finite lingered around our bodies, around the room, it enveloped the entire hotel, the town. But that day, that night, had already lasted for eons.

Her body was hot and I kissed her neck, cheek, lips, and I touched and massaged her breasts as she slid down onto her back. I began to tug at her jeans. I was *only* in my jeans. I had left my underwear crumpled in a corner next to my backpack. More smooching ensued. I pulled off her jeans. She helped. *She's so nice to help.* And then her body stilled. I was crouched over her, a steamroller in waiting. I kissed her neck, nibbled on her ear, but she'd become motionless. Something strange was afoot in room 700.

'What's the matter?' I whispered.

'David?'

'Yes?'

A low, exasperated sigh escaped from her mouth.

'Talk to me,' I said.

'I have to talk to you.'

'So talk to me.'

My gerbil started pounding the wheel between my temples. *Uh-oh. What's coming? What's coming? Please don't say that you're a man. It's happened to me before. Please don't say that you're a man. I wasn't that fucked up in Seattle, was I?*

'I'm a post-op transsexual, David.'

No! No! I didn't just fucking hear that! No...I didn't hear that.

There were more sighs. She was nervous, maybe embarrassed. But I could tell that she trusted me, thank god, she trusted me. And so, perched above her, I hovered, and waited, my head low, my ears wide open, expectant. *What's going to come?* She was flustered but she was going to tell me. Then she did.

'I...have...my period.' Her words trailed off, disappointed.

'Okay,' I said.

'I'm sorry,' she said.

'For what?'

'Listen...I don't know if I'm going to have sex with you this week. I don't know. This is all so strange.'

I hovered. I grinned. This woman was so fucking adorable. I was relieved. I'd thought it was going to be so much worse. I could handle this.

'It's alright, Samantha. I know this is very strange. But it's alright. I'm in no rush. I want you to be comfortable.'

She was frustrated, still a bit stiff, but slowly moving again.

'Yes...I'm sorry. I want to...but...'

My smile was huge. I was close to her head. I kissed her cheek, her neck. She expelled air from her nose in tight bursts. I invoked my baby voice.

Some women liked it. Some women thought it was annoying as hell. I thought Samantha could tolerate it. It was good for levity, and at that moment I thought we could use some levity.

'*I have my period,*' I cooed in my baby voice. She pushed me, playfully.

'Shut up.'

'*I have my period,*' I said again, breaking my hover. I moved across her breasts, down her stomach.

'Shut up.'

I spoke to her navel.

'I thought it was going to be something scary, dammit. Will you stop scaring me like that?'

'It *is* serious. Kind of.'

'I know...I know.'

I moved up her slender body and we kissed. And we kissed.

'I love you.'

'Stop saying that.'

'I love you.'

'You don't even know me.'

'I love you.'

'Don't you realize that I haven't returned the sentiment?'

'Yes...I know that. But—'

'But what?'

'I still love you.'

'Good god.'

'Yes.'

And as the minutes crept by and the pale moon moved across the sky, we giggled and spoke in low tones and we cuddled and we were tired and the day had been long. Samantha called her mother and lied about where she was—allegedly at my friend Mark's place and not room 700—but her mother made it very easy for her because her mother was very nice and the cool air pumped in through the vent by the window and we smoked a cigarette and doted on each other and petted and snuggled and cuddled and I was so warm being with her, amazing. Then sleep. Peaceful, peaceful, peaceful, safe, safe, safe. Beneath the spell of each other. How could I *not* love this woman?

***

'Ahhhh….chew!'

Bright yellow light exploded across the room to my nostrils. I woke up sneezing. *Motherfucker.*

It was morning, it was around 8:30 a.m., and we were in room 700 at the Radisson in Cambridge, Massachusetts and Samantha was sleeping next to me in my blue shirt that was now her blue shirt. I climbed out of bed and went to the window.

Wispy white clouds hung in the sky. The city was hazy. But it was bright out and it was Tuesday and we'd been together nearly a full day. I looked over my shoulder and Samantha was small and sleepy. I crept to the bathroom.

I made dirty hot water in the coffee maker and I smoked a cigarette and took another shower. Then I came out and sat in a chair across the room from Samantha and I drank my dirty tea and smoked another cigarette and watched her sleep. So happy. And I was still sneezing. *Motherfucker.*

I climbed back into bed next to her. I put my face in the pillow. She snored gently. I smiled into the pillow. She rolled over.

'Good morning, peaches,' I said, thinking, *Did I just say that? I think I did.*

'Good morning, my apple blossom.'

'Your mother left a message on my phone,' I whispered.

'Ohhh…' Samantha drowned herself in the blankets. 'I'm so sleepy.'

'You must be. I made some nasty hot water for tea.'

'Oh…Okay. I'm getting up.'

Samantha got up and shuffled around. I watched her, grinning. She was wearing my blue shirt and it was long, covering up those black panties with the red gun on the crotch that I so desperately wanted to steal. But they looked too good on her.

I must see them again someday, I thought. *Perhaps then I will destroy them in one violent snatch and tear. And then I'll devour them after dunking them in honey.*

I played her mother's message for her.

'I'm going to call her,' she said.

'Okay.'

I got up and opened the blinds. The room flooded with yellow. I sneezed more.

'What a view,' I said.

'Of what? Trader Joe's?'

So sarcastic. I love it.

'Fuck you,' I said. 'It *is* a nice view. You can see the city from here.'

As she called her mother, I snapped a couple of pictures out the window. I listened to her sweet little lies.

'Hi, Mom. Yeah, we're still at Mark's place...We'll be back shortly...'

She got off the phone and yawned. I snapped another picture, this time of her feet. We got our shit together and she called down to the front desk to check out.

'Tell them Eagle One is set for takeoff,' I said.

'Eagle One is set for takeoff,' she said into the phone. There was a pause and then, 'Oh, I mean, this is room 700 and we're leaving now...Is that better?'

We snagged a couple of matchbooks and scanned the room a last time before leaving. Then we left. But I'd taken pictures. I had the proof. We had really been there.

We drove out of Cambridge. It was sunny and hazy and warm and I was still wearing my fuzzy black fleece and my baseball hat and we listened to a live Martin Sexton CD. The CD opened with applause. I said, 'It's always good to wake up to applause.'

Samantha laughed. I called Mark again. It was too early to get lost.

'Mark?'

'What?'

He sounded sleepy too.

'How do I get to Hudson from Cambridge?'

He told me and I thanked him. Then he asked, 'So, did you fuck her?'

'Thanks, Mark.'

'Does that mean that you did or that you didn't?'

'Thanks, Mark. You're a lifesaver.'

'You're such a fucking idiot.'

We made it back to Hudson without incident. I smoked, she smoked, we held hands in the truck. We were slow, maybe a little sad. But I was coming back later in the week. There was no way that I wasn't. We stopped at Dunkin' Donuts in Hudson. Samantha made fun of it.

'This place sucks.'

'No, *you* suck.'

We bought donuts, water, coffee and chocolate milk.

We drove back to Ledgewood. I was sweating and my nose was filled with snot. We went up the cement steps and onto the porch. Samantha's mother answered the door in a slinky robe, already trying to entice me.

'Hello,' Samantha said, and when she turned her head, her mother winked at me, slyly. I blushed. We moved inside.

'How was your night?' her mother asked.

'It was nice,' Samantha said. 'Mark lives in a mansion.'

Her mother nodded, wide eyed and impressed. She stole another moment to wink at me and pat me on the behind. I was bright red by now.

We moved back to the porch and ate our snacks. I drank my chocolate milk slowly, savoring the taste. Samantha's mother sipped at the coffee. Samantha shoved two whole donuts into her mouth and tried to talk. It was disturbing.

'Mmmuh wahhh muuu, ha ha ha!'

She laughed at her own joke. No one else got it.

Her mother got up and went back inside. She had to get dressed. Samantha had to shower. She never took advantage of the shower at the hotel. I had to leave.

I followed her back in, hooking my fingers in the pockets of her jeans. I wanted to pull them off. Samantha's mother appeared again, still in robe. She was procrastinating getting dressed. She was such a tease.

'Thank you for letting me steal your daughter,' I said.

'You can *have* her,' she said.

Samantha feigned alarm.

'Hey!'

And while Samantha bugged out, her mother mouthed these words to me:

You can have me too, you dirty fucker.

***

'I have to go now.'

'I know.'

'You have to clean up.'

'I know.'

'You have to visit your uncle.'

'I know.'

Mel Bosworth

'But I'll be back.'

'Yeah?'

'You know I'll be back.'

'I'm so glad that you came.'

'I'm so glad that you came.'

This isn't over. Not even close.

Outside, we embraced. She was strong, warm. My beak was sweating.

'Your mother is awesome.'

'She didn't try to hit on you, did she?'

I remembered our pact.

'No....of course not.'

Samantha eyed me warily and then said, 'Okay.'

We kissed. I was so in love with her. She hadn't returned the sentiment yet, but I understood. I had to go.

'I have to go now.'

'Okay.'

'I'm going to call you tonight.'

'Call me tonight.'

'I will.'

'Okay.'

We laughed nervously, sadly.

Samantha said, 'I had a great time. Thank you.'

I said, 'I had a great time. Thank you.'

My heart was heavy. But I'd be back in a couple of days. We knew this. Samantha was in

Massachusetts and we knew this. We embraced again. My fingers lingered on her skin.

'I'll call you tonight,' I said.

'Call me tonight.'

'Good luck this afternoon.'

Samantha rolled her hazel eyes.

'Yeah, I know.'

We were still under the spell. I loved this woman to death. This made no sense. It made complete sense. I had to go.

'I have to go.'

'I know.'

'I'll call you tonight.'

'Call me tonight.'

I moved to my truck. She watched me. I watched her. I backed out of the narrow driveway. She watched. She waved. I watched. I waved. I could still see her through the branches. I honked. Happy honk. I was smitten with her. Then I couldn't see her anymore. I bit my lip and drove. I drove back home.

The Pike was busy but moving, bright but not blurring. I cranked my live Martin Sexton CD and pounded the air around me, jubilant.

The week moved dazedly. I was dazedly. I was happy. Oh, so happy. Samantha was busying herself in Hudson and Boston with her mother, shopping and touring, visiting her uncle with the broken leg in Benton. I talked to her every night.

During the day I got beat up at work but I didn't care. I worked for a small landscaping company and it was getting late in the season. The work hours were diminishing and soon I'd get laid off for the winter, but with Samantha so close the timing couldn't have been better.

One day I got into a fight with a rose bush and the rose bush won, shredding my forearms. The next day I got into a fight with a heavy socket wrench and the socket wrench won, defeating my collarbone. But I took the scratches and the bruises in stride; I was happy. During those days, I often thought to myself, *These fuckers could beat me with lead pipes and I wouldn't care. I'm happy. Samantha is so close. She is so close.*

The week was perfect. Samantha and her mother had picked a perfect week to come to Massachusetts, busted up Uncle aside. It was an oddly mild week in November and most of the leaves had fallen. The days were yellow and temperate and the nights dark and crisp.

Friday evening, the sun was setting as I drove back to Hudson. I wasn't as nervous this time but I was still nervous but not like I had been. I was wearing my olive and orange fleece that I'd bought for a couple of bucks from a thrift store. And I was wearing jeans and my running shoes.

I drove east on the Massachusetts turnpike. I hadn't spoken to Mark since this latest outing began and I didn't plan to. Mark had helped me enough this week. He was such a good friend. He hated my guts.

I took exit 21 and then 20 North and then I was in Hudson. It was busy and I moved through the center slowly. The sky was dark but the street and the sidewalks glowed. Yellow headlights and red brake lights and strings of white lights in the windows of the restaurants bars and stores and lots of couples were out and about, young men and women looking very nice, doing up the big town, walking arm in arm or hand in hand and I was happy that I had a girlfriend. I smiled through town.

Moon then Main then Chess then Ledgewood. I was such a fucking pro now. I had this thing down pat. I pulled up the driveway of her uncle's house and shut off the truck. I got out and walked up steps. I cranked a funny little crank on the door and it made a funny little sound. The door opened.

'Hey.'

It was bright inside the house. The porch was dim. Shadows and light. Meeting Samantha, once more, with the light at her back, making her edges glow, making her even more angelic than I remembered, made me crazier, more obsessive, and more ridiculous than I'd ever been. This woman owned me.

'Hey,' I said. Then, 'Wow. You look amazing.'

She flipped her hair, blushing. 'Oh, shut up.'

She had broken out the black string bikini this evening. Around her neck hung a black silk choker and on her feet were black six inch heels. She was as tall as me. Her hair was down and she had rings on her fingers. She invited me inside and we embraced, and she smelled good, like fresh flowers, and I closed my eyes and squeezed her body and I could feel the bikini melt away. I stepped back and she was wearing a white tank top, tight jeans and worn leather boots. I stared at my jeans and sneakers, feeling very underdressed.

'I look like a fuck,' I lamented. 'You look amazing.'

'No, no,' Samantha assured. 'You look fine.'

Somewhere in the corners of the house I could hear her mother moving. Then she came into view. At first I didn't recognize her. And then I did. I was looking at Sissy Spacek, the actress.

'What...?'

She was taller and she was wearing glasses but she wore glasses anyway and her hair was long and straight and her eyes were blue and I was looking at Sissy Spacek from her role in David Lynch's 'The Straight Story.' I was stunned. Samantha giggled, knowingly.

'Trim-Spa,' her mother explained. I rubbed my eyes. Then, to my right, Samantha began to play the Trim-Spa theme on a shining saxophone. The hallway filled with sound and I stared at Samantha and her mother stared too, and her face was proud as she watched and listened.

Samantha leaned back and her lips embraced the reed, and she played and played with such emotion and then she finished and cleared the spit-valve and a wad of saliva landed on the hardwood floor and we all stared at it, wondering what it could possibly mean. Samantha's mother and I broke into applause.

'Wonderful!' Sissy exclaimed.

Samantha bowed and set the sax on a small table at the bottom of the staircase. I noticed then that Charlie Parker's signature had been etched into it. I wondered, *Did Bird play alto or tenor?*

Samantha's mother/Sissy Spacek told us that we should go, that the night was young and so were we. Samantha grabbed me by my elbow and my toe and flipped me over her shoulder.

'Let's go.'

Such a brute. Such brute force. It's very sexy.

Sissy applauded the fact that I was draped over her daughter's shoulder. We turned toward the front door.

'Get the knob,' ordered Samantha.

I turned the knob. Then she hooked the door with her foot and pulled it open. It clipped my head.

'Ouch.'

'Stop being such a pussy. If I don't carry you to this restaurant we're never going to get out of this house. I mean, really—playing the sax in the hallway? Why do you write such drivel?'

I could smell her hair, her head. She was aromatic, sweet.

I said, 'It's not drivel. It's fitting. It's a little bit of everything that we've talked about. I'm showcasing your *talents*.'

We thumped down the cement steps. My head hurt with each thump.

'My *talents*? I haven't played the sax in years,' said Samantha. 'If you want to showcase my talents, why don't you write a scene where I kick your motherfucking ass and then scalp you?'

'You're soooo Native American,' I said.

She was German and Native American.

'You like that, huh?'

'You could scalp me anytime.'

Sissy Spacek waved from the doorway.

'Bye bye, kids!'

Samantha turned and so I turned too. I was draped over her shoulder.

'Bye, Mom!'

'Bye, Sissy!'

'Bye, kids!'

We were a pack of waving morons and then the door swung closed and we moved down the driveway.

'Can you set me down now?'

'Are you going to get us to the restaurant?'

'If you want me to.'

'I want you to.'

'Then let's go to the restaurant.'

'Fine.'

Samantha shrugged me off of her shoulder and I landed on my feet.

'Thank you.'

'You're welcome.'

'I love you.'

'What the fuck did I tell you about that?'

'Right.'

We walked to the center of Hudson. It wasn't far. Later, on the way home, we'd take a cab but neither of us would remember it very well. We held hands as we walked. Things had settled back to normal.

'David?'

'Yes?'

'Do you think we'll ever get married?'

'I don't know. That's a good question.'

'But do you think it's a possibility?'

'Anything is possible,' I said.

We looked at each other and smiled and I pulled her close. We were now a single entity walking toward the center of Hudson—two heads, four arms, four legs, a penis and a vagina. Neighborhood children ran from us in fear. Car horns honked, people screamed. German, Native American, English, Polish, and whatever the fuck else we could cram into our monster suit we crammed in, and as we shuffled down the sidewalk we grunted like animals, letting our proverbial freak flag fly. At one point, as we stood at a crosswalk waiting for the light to change, we decided to wag our tongues and make our eyes real big and—

Samantha smacked the back of the head.

'What the fuck did I tell you? Restaurant? Please?'

'Right...Sorry.'

Arm in arm in the moist but comfortable night air, we made our way down and then up and we were at the restaurant. It was Cambodian. Samantha had been there before, earlier in the week with her mother. This was her night to plan. This was our second date. I trusted her completely. We stood outside, smoking. Inside, a few people chattered and chewed. It was past eight o'clock. We went inside.

The room was small but spacious, the walls painted a soothing color like rust or earth tones and everything was soft and textured and the tables were ample and the wait staff friendly and accommodating. We were led through an easy maze to a table in the back against the wall. Samantha took the seat looking out. I took the seat looking in.

'This place is very cool,' I said.

'I came here the other day with my mother. It's sooo good.'

It smelled good. Almost as good as Samantha. A man came over to give us menus and to take our drink orders.

'I'll have a red wine,' said Samantha.

Ooooh! I thought. *What class! What charm!* I knew she really wanted a Pabst Blue Ribbon but was just afraid to ask.

'I'll have a Jack and Coke,' I said.

I really wanted a Pabst Blue Ribbon too.

Our drink selection was as cool as we were. We knew this. We could see it in each other's eyes. Hazel and brown. Her eyes were so hypnotic. We began to play an easy game of footsie under the table. It was hot in the restaurant. A waiter came over and adjusted the thermostat.

'Make it cooler,' I said, still wearing my fleece, wondering why I was hot.

He looked over and nodded.

'Hot in here, right?' he asked.

'Yes,' Samantha and I said together, again the mishmash monster of limbs and genitalia.

'Is it humid out?' asked the waiter.

'Kind of,' I said.

'Well that would explain it. It gets hot in here when it's humid out.'

Then he whistled the theme song to 'Taxi.' Samantha squealed with joy.

'I love that tune!'

'I know you do!'

Then her face became very serious. It made me serious.

'David?'

'Yes?'

'How do you think part four is coming along?'

'I'm not too confident about it.'

'Why not?'

'Well…'

I stared off into space. I could get lost in the décor of the restaurant. I said, 'It's just that I keep getting fucked up as I try to write this, and I know that it's important, maybe even more important than the beginning of the week, and I don't know. I don't think I'm capturing it very well.'

'I think it's okay.'

'Yeah? You really do?'

Samantha reached across the table and took my hand. Soft but strong.

'I do,' she said, and then she smiled and it made me smile.

'Thank you for lying,' I said.

A waitress came over. She had a Silly Putty face and her neck was covered in hickies.

'Ready to order?' she asked.

I pointed to Samantha.

'I'll have the Alabama Gumbo,' she said. 'And could we get some spring rolls too?'

The waitress scribbled onto a pad. She looked at me.

'I'll have the Crazy Fish on a Plate,' I said.

She scribbled more.

'Alright,' she said. 'Thank you.'

'Thanks.'

'Thanks.'

She left and the room got very loud. I was staring at the wall. Samantha could see the room. I wished for a moment that we could live here in the restaurant, raising our children on Alabama Gumbo and Crazy Fish on a Plate. We could make our clothes out of tablecloths and we could home school the children. I sipped on my drink. Samantha sipped on hers.

'I like this place a lot,' I said. 'Thank you for taking me here.'

'It's awesome. The food here is awesome.'

'You're awesome.'

'I know. You're awesome too.'

We were adorable, just like a real couple, just like real people. I wanted to tear off her shirt. I entertained ideas behind my eyes.

'Tell me about your other girlfriends,' she said.

'Tell me about your other boyfriends.'

We traded some war stories. We traded the good and the bad. We were traders. It was all very informative. I watched her as she spoke. She often grew very excited, her hands moving fast. Her eyes, those hazel eyes, were hypnotic. Our food came.

'Alabama Gumbo for the sweet lady and Crazy Fish on a Plate for the gentleman. And spring rolls. Does the amazing couple need any more drinks?'

'Yes.'

'Yes.'

We ate. I secretly choked on a piece of bone. I'd choke on it for hours and learn to ignore it. Samantha had a pyramid of noodles and other colorful things and a huge bowl of white rice sat on the edge of the small table. I told her I wanted to throw rice at her.

'Please don't.'

'Okay.'

My Crazy Fish tasted like butter and spices. We shared Crazy Fish and noodles. Ravi Shankar played a sitar in the background. Samantha took out her camera. I put on the blinders, hands at my eyes. She took a picture, careful to get the both of us in frame.

We ate, we laughed, we told stories. She had dated some interesting men. I had dated some interesting women. My beak was sweating. Samantha pointed this out.

'I know,' I said. 'My nose sweats when I'm drinking.'

'I think it's cute.'

'I think you're cute.'

Then the room got very loud and I had to yell. Samantha had to yell. Then the room got very quiet.

'Is it empty now?' I asked.

'Yes, kind of.'

Our food was shredded and scattered about the table. We sipped our drinks. Samantha's wine glass was very delicate, the stem long and thin. We pooled our collective wisdom garnered from insane relationships. We knew what we liked and we knew what we didn't like. We knew that we liked each other. The check came.

'I got this one, my little monkey,' I said.

Samantha frowned and looked pretty but she ended up covering the tip. She was an easy feminist. I liked that. Girly but strong, opinionated but open to new ideas. We said 'Thanks' to the wait staff and they said 'Thanks' back and we went outside.

We stood on the sidewalk and lit cigarettes.

'That was awesome.'

'That was awesome.'

'What now?' I asked.

'Let's go this way.'

We walked arm in arm back the way we came. Samantha had seen a bar up the road. It was Friday night and the Celtics were playing the Knicks at Madison Square Garden. It was close to ten o'clock. We could catch the end of the game and cuddle in a booth. I liked this idea. We smiled and held hands as we walked.

'What do you think?' I asked.

'About?'

'Four?'

Samantha considered the question. Then she said, 'It's alright. I think I might've done things a bit different, though.'

'Oh yeah? Like what?'

'Maybe put in more of our conversations.'

I nodded, slowly.

'Yeah. You're probably right. I was having a hard time just getting through this.'

'*Probably*?'

'Probably what?'

'*Probably right*? You know I'm fucking right.'

She was beautiful. I felt like such a slug again.

'Okay. You're right.'

She elbowed me playfully in the ribs. I wrapped her in my arms and we kissed. Our faces close, she whispered, 'End this piece of garbage already, my love. Take me to five.'

And she was right; she was so right. I could see it all over her face, her body. Samantha was right. Samantha was right in ways that I didn't even know yet. We closed our eyes and we kissed. Car horns honked, people screamed, children ran from us in a mixture of terror and awe. My eyes closed and our foreheads pressed together I whispered,

'I...am...so...in—'

'Shhh.'

'I...am...so...in...love—'

'Shhh. Take me to five, David. Take me to five.'

Her voice was soothing. It stopped my disintegration into a bumbling moron. I nodded and collected myself, my thoughts. I opened my eyes. Samantha was looking right at me, right into my brain and then beyond. I tried to match her power. But I was still weak.

'Five?' I asked.

'Five.'

'Okay. Are *you* ready for five?'

She nodded.

'Yes. I think so.'

'I won't make it bad, I promise.'

Her eyes were nervous and searching. She would do some interesting things in five, things that even *I* wouldn't remember very well. I touched her cheek and then kissed it. I was getting stronger now. Samantha needed me to be strong. I whispered in her ear

'Ready?'

'Okay.'

'We'll be fine.'

'Okay.'

And with bellies full of wine and whiskey and fish and noodles and rice, we made our way down the sidewalk toward five, the number of chaos, and our heads were held high and we were together and our fingers were interlaced, and my beak was still sweating, and Samantha looked beautiful, and nothing could harm us. The lampposts were jealous as we glided by.

one two three four **FIVE** six

A crowd had gathered on the sidewalk outside the bar.

'Is that the line to get in?' asked Samantha.

'Yes. No. I think everyone is just smoking. Good ol' Massachusetts.'

We sidestepped through the throng of smokers and went inside. The room was filled with cheers and jeers and lots of dark polished wood and high backed booths. Several screens around the room showed the end of the basketball game. The Celtics were losing. We moved to the far end of the bar.

'What are you drinking?' I asked.

Samantha told me. Then she ran off to the bathroom. I was left alone at the edge of the bar. I snaked a fifty from my wallet. The bartender was slow, preoccupied with nothing. Finally, our eyes caught.

'I'll take a this and a that,' I said.

He nodded and moved off. Samantha returned and wrapped her arms around my waist. We looked up at the screens and waited for the drinks. They came and we moved off to a booth in the corner.

I held onto Samantha's thigh. She pressed close to me. We were a couple. We were giddy with alcohol and Crazy Fish on a Plate. We were giddy with each other. We sipped and cuddled and watched the game. The crowd inside was antsy, shaky. The Celtics were losing and we were inside a bar just outside of Boston. We needed shots of something.

'Shots?' I asked.

'Okay. What?'

'You pick.'

'Not tequila. I go nuts when I drink tequila.'

Hmmm...Maybe we should get some tequila.

'Ok,' I said. 'How about a wimpy shot? Something like a red-headed slut or a grape-crush?'

'What's in that?'

'I'm not sure. But they're both easy.'

We got shots. I downed mine in one motion. Samantha sipped hers. She was so classy. The blood rushed to our faces. Our ears and noses were red and our lips wet. We were drunks. Two drunks sitting in a bar. We were partners in crime.

The Celtics were losing. They were down ten with less than a minute to go. A little blue eyed waitress came over to the booth. She bowed. We were the King and the Queen of the bar. Everyone knew it. We knew it.

'Are you two alright over here?'

I pointed to our glasses.

'Fire it up?' I asked.

She nodded.

'Do you want to start a tab?'

'Perfect.'

The waitress went away. A woman paced back and forth back and forth in front of us, often covering her face with her hands. On the screen, Paul Pierce was at the line shooting free throws. Some smartass in the room said, 'Don't fucking miss.'

And Pierce missed but it didn't matter anyway. The Celtics were going to lose. *Fuck it.* I squeezed Samantha's leg.

'How are you doing?' I asked.

'I'm fine. This is so much fun.'

'It's too bad the Celtics are losing, though. This place is gonna be mad when they lose.'

'Yeah.'

'Another shot?'

'Okay.'

I looked around for our waitress. She had disappeared. I got up.

'I'm going to get shots at the bar. Our waitress is cute, but she's slow.'

'Okay.'

'I'll be right back.'

'I love you, David.'

'I know.'

I went to the bar. I flagged the bartender and ordered. He nodded and proceeded to move to the far end of the bar where he could lean. He sucked on a few limes and stared off into space. *What the fuck?* I thought. He was leaning and sucking for so long that I thought he had already forgotten my order. I gave him the crazy eyes and he kind of nodded slowly, as if waking from a daydream. *What a fuck.*

I watched Samantha over the tops of the booths. She was sitting, smiling, all alone at our big table in our big booth. I tried to get her attention by making silly faces but she didn't look over at me. It was okay. I could play the voyeur. It was how we'd met. I'd been watching her. I watched her now.

Our ears and noses were red and our lips wet. Two drunks in a bar. The shots came.

'Thanks, you fucking piece of shit,' I mumbled.

'What was that?'

'I said, *Thanks, I've got to take my seat.*'

'Whatever, man.'

He offered me a lime to suck on. I ignored him and walked away with the shots. I slid next to Samantha.

'Hey,' I said.

'Hey.'

'Did I miss anything?'

Samantha pointed to the pacing woman.

'That woman is bugging out.'

'Big Celtics fan,' I said.

'Oh yeah.'

'Shot?'

'Yeah.'

We drank our shots. I downed mine in one motion. Samantha sipped hers. She was so classy. The Celtics lost. People whined.

'Fuck.'

'Bullshit.'

'That sucked. Let's scram.'

'Nice work, Pierce.'

'Fuck fuck fuck.'

'Bullshit bullshit bullshit.'

But we were still smiling, the King and the
Queen. I was glad that Samantha got to see some
of a Celtics game so close to Boston, even if they
did lose. The other patrons tucked their tails
between their legs and poured out onto the
sidewalk and the street. The room grew quiet.
Then Depeche Mode began to pump through the
speakers. I liked this bar. Samantha liked it too.

'I love Depeche Mode,' she said.

'Me too. Violator is their best album.'

Samantha stared at me then with eyes filled with
love and alcohol. She bit her lip. I wanted to bite
them too.

'Who *are* you?' she asked. 'Most guys hate
Depeche Mode.'

I'm not most guys.

'I like good music,' I explained. 'Depeche Mode
is good music.'

Two drunks in a bar. Two drunks in love in a
bar. In Hudson. Just outside of Boston. Our
waitress returned.

'How late are you open?' Samantha asked.

It was the classic alcoholic question. I loved that.

'Until one,' said the waitress. 'You've got plenty
of time.'

'Great.'

'Drinks?' she asked.

Mel Bosworth

'Yes, please.'

The waitress left and we talked. The bar was wide open, calm. Samantha told me more crazy stories about the men she'd dated. I told her more crazy stories about the women I'd dated. We liked to trade crazy stories, just like at the restaurant, only now we offered more detail. We were getting drunk, loose. I was squeezing her thigh. She pressed close to me. We got up and went outside to have a cigarette. And as we were dancing on the sidewalk, a group of heavy New York accents came spilling toward us. They were drunk, a bit rowdy.

'Hey. Let's go inside this bar.'

'Nah. It's dead. Look at it. It's dead.'

'No one is in there.'

'We're in there,' we said.

We were wearing our monster suit again. Arms, legs, penis, vagina. Two heads. They loved Samantha immediately. They had to be cordial to me because I was with her, but they'd kill me given the chance.

'And who are *you*?' asked a bloke wearing a rugby shirt.

'I'm Samantha. I'm from Washington. I'm hot. I'm always right.'

*She never says that. I don't know why I keep writing it. I
must think it's funny.*

Rugby guy told us they were visiting from New
York. Then we all went inside the bar. They
offered to buy us drinks. We had a posse now. We
took up stools. We got drinks. We chatted with our
new friends. We took some pictures. They quickly
learned that we were the King and Queen of the
bar. They were our servants. They worked for us.
We were Gods. Our ears and noses were red and
our lips wet. We were drunks. We were in love.

'Who wants a shot of green monkey piss?'
someone asked.

'I do!'

'I do!'

'I do!'

Samantha was one of the first 'I do's' and I
looked over to her, surprised. She had turned into
party girl. I loved this. The New York posse, who
had come with a girl but who was dust compared
to Samantha, loved this too. They were in love
with Samantha. They wanted to cut my throat.

We slammed a row of shots. I tossed a twenty at
someone and someone else ordered more drinks. I
was drinking Jack Daniel's through a straw. I had
been for some time.

Music and drinks and *we* were the bar now, our

group of miscreants and would be murderers. We sang and laughed and a mountain of muscle sat next to Samantha and me after we motioned for him to come closer to the King and Queen. He told us a story.

'Guess who we fucking saw tonight?' he asked.

'Tom Brady?' I guessed.

'No. But you're on the right track.'

'Josh Beckett?'

'Yes. Fucking Josh Beckett. He was at the liquor store buying five gallons of Hennessey. He had a hood up and he was pretending he was talking on his cell phone the whole time. What a dick.'

These guys hated everything about Boston sports teams. They were from New York. It was their birthright to hate Boston. But they needed us, just like we needed them. Samantha fanned herself with a menu.

'I forgot to tell you something,' she whispered to me.

'What?'

'I forgot to tell you about the dancing.'

The dancing…The dancing? What does that mean? Was she a stripper in Seattle? How did I miss that one? But no. Samantha just loved to dance. And so she danced.

'Oh my god,' someone said.

'Look at this.'

'That dude is the luckiest guy in here.'

'Let's fucking kill him.'

'Oh my god.'

A small guy in a paisley shirt that reminded me of something from my own wardrobe pushed me. His name was Phil.

'Go dance with her!'

I shook my head.

'No way. I'm watching this just like you guys.

Phil pushed me again.

'Go dance with her!'

'No way. Out of my realm of possibility. I'd ruin it for everyone.'

Phil cheered. Samantha danced for us. Her dark hair whirled. Her hips swayed while her white smile illuminated the bronzed, glistening flesh of her face. But she stopped dancing after getting everyone excited and then she fell into me, laughing, smiling. Our ears and noses were red and our lips wet. We kissed.

'You're awesome,' I told her.

'I love to dance!'

'You're awesome.'

Then someone came over to me and whispered into my ear, 'Dude, we've decided...we're going to kill you and kidnap your girlfriend.'

'Please don't.'

'Well, we'll see.'

Good enough. I had bought myself some time. Now I had to make more friends. I bought more drinks. Someone else bought more drinks. Everyone's ears and noses were red and everyone's lips were wet. We were all drunk. The cute waitress appeared at my side and I settled up our tab from earlier.

'More green monkey piss!' someone boomed.

And so we lined up more shots. We drank them. Then we lined up more. We drank them. We were caving in. We were caving in fast.

Do we need to settle up any more with the horrid bartender? I wondered. Last call had come and gone. The lights were coming up now. Phil was making some bad noise with the blonde, shithead bartender. More money flew. We left a tip of some sort. We were nice to the waitress. *Fuck the bartender.* But we tipped him anyway. Then, the street.

Everything was tunnel vision. *Were we in the street? No, we were in an alleyway next to the bar.* The air was thick. It was dark out. Shadows and light. Samantha squatted next to a dumpster. I followed suit and pissed on a metal staircase.

Did we say goodbye to the New York posse? I

wondered. I didn't know. It didn't matter. *Job well done.*

Samantha had become a puppet without strings. She was floppy. So floppy. And beautiful. I could see this through my tunnel vision. She was crying. Her bag was on the ground. I slung it across my chest.

'Baby, what's the matter?' I asked.

'I don't...I don't want you to go.'

She was crying. I held her face.

'Look at me.'

She looked up at me with wet hazel eyes. Our ears and noses were red and our lips wet.

'I'm right here,' I said. 'I'm right in front of you. I'm not going anywhere.'

'Really?'

'Yes.'

We kissed. Then I was beckoned by a dull sense of responsibility.

'But we have to get out of here,' I said. 'We have to get a cab.'

Samantha flailed her arms. She pushed me off.

'No. Get off of me.'

'It's okay. Listen, we have to get out of here. You need to pull it together for just a few minutes, okay?'

There was more flailing. I wasn't sure if she

recognized me anymore. She sat on the ground. She smoked a cigarette. I stepped out of the alley and onto the sidewalk. I waved down a taxi. I opened the back door and stuck my head inside.

'It'll be just a second, buddy. Just hang on. I'll pay.'

'Whatever.'

I ran back into the alley and tried to scoop up Samantha. She was floppy, uncooperative. It was madness but I loved it.

'The cab is waiting,' I tried to tell her. 'We've got to go now.'

'What? Fuck off.'

Gravity was having its way with her body. She would sleep in the alley if I let her. But I couldn't do that. The New York boys must have been nearby, waiting to see if I'd leave her. But I wasn't going to. She was my girlfriend. And so we wrestled. I won. I pulled her into my tunnel vision and we made it into the back of the cab. She slumped against the door, her head low.

'Ledgewood,' I slurred.

The car moved. I blacked out for a moment in the backseat. When I opened my eyes, we were moving up Ledgewood and it was dark out and quiet.

'Stop right here!' I yelled.

The car came to a fast stop. I'd startled the driver. He must have thought we were dead. We were stopped at the end of the street. I tried to stir Samantha. She was making wet drunken sounds. She was wasted. So was I. But someone had to run this show.

'C'mon, baby. We're here. We have to get out now.'

I opened the back door.

'How much, buddy?' I asked.

'MMmmmmuuuussssshhh,' said the driver.

I had no fucking clue what he said.

'Sounds good, my man.'

I shoved a twenty in his direction, maybe more, maybe less. I was confident that whatever I gave him would cover it. It was a short ride. Samantha was resisting me again. Then suddenly she was lucid.

'Where the fuck is my bag?'

'I have it. It's right here across my chest.'

She sighed drunken relief.

'We have to get out now, baby,' I said.

There were grumbles and grunts, what the fucks and assholes and growls. She got out of the car. Or maybe I pulled her out of the car. We stood in the street. She stumbled in slow motion onto a grassy bank: the front of someone's lawn. The door of the cab was still open. I quickly assessed the situation and realized that I had to close the door. And so I did.

'Thanks, pal.'

Then I ran over to the lawn where Samantha had crashed. I worried that she would hit her head on the road. She was taking her clothes off.

'What are you…?'

Fuck it. I helped her take her clothes off. I took off my own clothes. We kissed and rolled around and the ground was soft and cool and we were in the grass and in the leaves and twigs and I pulled off her pants and then her panties and I went down on her and got a mouthful of leaves and I spat them out and I thought, *This is so bad…We have to get out of here,* but we weren't stopping.

'We have to get out of here.'

Kiss, smooch, Kiss.

'We can't be here. This is so fucking bad. We're on the side of the road, baby.'

Kiss, smooch, Kiss.

Samantha was completely naked. So was I. We were fucking on a lawn. Then we were fucking on the side of the road. I looked at her tits, soft and white, under the streetlight. I worried about her head again. She was half in/ half out of the road.

This is bad. We can't be here.

Then a red car rolled by. It rolled by slowly. We were naked and fucking in the road and on a lawn. It was late. It was dark.

I bet that car heard us and wanted to see the show. Come to think of it, I'm pretty sure I saw lights come on at the house we were terrorizing so they must have got a good show too. Thank god no one called the cops. Thank god. They probably would've brought Samantha home and I'd be in the clink on rape charges. But…people know love when they see it. We were in love.

We stopped. We had to stop. I pulled Samantha out of the road. She was spaghetti. I almost dropped her. I was getting wavy now too. The green monkey piss was racing through my system. I was failing fast, melting. We had to get out of there before something went wrong.

'Samantha, you have to pull it together. We have to get out of here.'

'No.'

'C'mon.'

I tried to round up our clothes. I was having a hard time finding everything. I got my pants and my shirt and my shoes on and fuck—I couldn't find my cell phone. That was bad.

Where the fuck is it?

I sparked my lighter and tip toed around the

lawn in search of my phone. Samantha was still naked, sitting, lying. I found my phone, miraculously, pressed down in the grass. Then I found her purse. I slung it across my chest. Then I found her pants. Then her shirt. Then her little long sleeved hoodie. I pulled her over to me and started to dress her. It was hard work. Samantha didn't resist, but she didn't help either. Finally, I got her pants on. Then the hoodie. I stuffed her shirt and bra into my back pockets. We were almost ready to move. Then she pulled off all of her clothes again. I was exasperated, but patient.

'Samantha.'

'No.'

'C'mon.'

'No.'

We went through the routine again. Pants on, then hoodie. We were covered in leaves and twigs. We were almost ready. Samantha started to take off the hoodie. I stopped her this time.

'Samantha, listen to me. It's late. We're on the side of the road. We can't be here anymore. We have to go back to the house. We have to leave this place. What I need you to do is pull it together, just for a few minutes so we can get inside. You can do this. *You can do this.*'

Her head was low and her hair was full of leaves

and twigs. I still had a hard on. She looked up at me and smiled. Then she said, 'No.'

Fuck it, I thought. *I'm not fighting with her anymore. We need action. We need to elude the police, the neighborhood watch.* And so I pulled her to her feet.

'Ready?'

'No.'

'Here we go.'

I moved Samantha up the street. I didn't have to carry her. Once her body was set in motion, it remembered how to walk, and so it did. It didn't walk *well* the whole way, but her body was walking, and I was holding onto her, and she was slowly coming to the surface of the alcohol, she was slowly coming back to me.

'We're so fucked,' I said.

'I don't want you to go.'

'I'm not going anywhere.'

We made it to her uncle's house. We made it up the cement steps. We were trying to be hushed. We stood on the porch and I gave Samantha her bag. She fumbled around, looking for the keys to the house. She couldn't find them. Then the door opened. I shrunk so fast, I became nothing.

I'm such a fucking asshole.

Samantha lit up like a pinball machine. Her mother/Sissy Spacek stood in the doorway.

'What are you kids doing?' she asked.

She's been awake for a while, I thought. *She's been watching our show.*

I was tiny, hiding inside of myself. Samantha recoiled to this new scene like she'd been hit with ice water. I was small but Samantha was back from oblivion.

'I couldn't find the keys,' she said, surprisingly straight all of a sudden. I kept my head and my eyes low. We had to get inside. We had to get past Sissy. We had to get out of sight. The cops were on their way, they had to be.

'Well, get in here, you fucking idiots,' Sissy said, stepping aside.

We stumbled inside. I tried to keep my front to Sissy so she wouldn't see the clothes hanging from my back pockets.

'Sorry, sorry,' I mumbled.

I moved past Sissy and followed Samantha into the studio. Sissy trailed us, questioning.

'It's four in the morning. Where have you two been?'

Samantha stood in the shadows of the studio, flipping her hair. Leaves and twigs showered down from our bodies.

'We met these kids,' she said. 'They wanted to kidnap me but David wouldn't let them.'

'Eh?'

Sissy looked at me. I nodded, idiotically.

'That's right,' I said. 'But we're fine. Took the long way home is all.'

'I see.'

More leaves and twigs seasoned the floor. Sissy rolled her eyes and threw up her hands. I sat on a little couch in the studio with my hands on my thighs, trying to play it cool. Samantha ran upstairs to get blankets, leaving me alone with Sissy.

'Are you going to be alright down here, David?' she asked.

'Yes, yes,' I said. 'This will be fine. Thank you for letting me crash here.'

'Oh, it's not a problem. Well, good night.'

'Yes, thank you. Good night.'

Sissy left. Samantha returned with blankets and sat down next to me. We started to kiss. We stopped to snap a picture. We moved to the floor. We were fucked. Our ears and noses were red and our lips wet.

I got up and turned off the lights. The sun was coming up and the room was glowing with dawn. Wrapped in blankets, we lay on the carpet in the studio, uncomfortable, kissing, hugging. We tried to have sex again. But we were fucked now worse than before. The alcohol wouldn't release us. I had a condom somewhere, miles away. I didn't care.

And so we tried to have sex, with varying degrees of success. My knees got rug burned. I had trouble staying hard. Samantha's cookie was dry as a bone. I decided to go down on her but it didn't help much. And so I fucked her with my hand and stuck my tongue up her ass. She was awake, making noises, but our ship was sinking and this wasn't happening. And so we fumbled around and fucked it up and then we passed out.

A few hours later, it was nine in the morning and Samantha was awake. She and Sissy were driving to the Cape soon and I had to leave. We were still wasted.

'You *can't* leave today.'

'I think I have to.'

My hat was pulled low over my eyes.

'But you *can't* leave today.'

'I think I have to.'

Samantha and I were sitting out on the stoop. It was 9:30 a.m. on Saturday and although we were somewhat awake and functional, we were still drunk. Our eyes were glassy and we were dirty and the occasional twig would spill from some part of our monster suit. We were close and giddy and laughing. Samantha was pressed into my side, speaking feverishly.

'Listen. I have a plan.'

'Okay.'

'I'm going to tell my mother that I don't want to

go to the Cape today. She can go alone. We can hang out at the house all day.'

'And we can have sex?'

'*All day*. In every room.'

This sounded like an amazing idea. But I was doubtful. This was bad. This was so bad. Samantha's mother had been planning their Cape Cod trip for weeks. They would only be in Hudson for three more days.

'You think your mom will go for it?'

'Yes. She *has* to.'

'So…what do we do?'

I could hear the gerbil spinning frantically behind Samantha's hazel eyes as she cooked up the plan.

'Well, I'll do all the talking. But you have to back me up.'

'And how do I do that?'

'You just have to stand next to me, looking adorable.'

I frowned and weighed things in my head. Then I asked, 'Sex? All day?'

'Yes.'

'Really?'

'In every fucking room. I'm going to eat you alive.'

'Do you mean it?'

'Yes.'

'If you think you can pull it off.'

'I can. We have to do this.'

The stoop was cold. The sun was coming up in the east. The tops of the pine trees were orange. Ledgewood was sleepy. But the scent of our crimes lingered about the neighborhood like the scent of burnt toast in a kitchen. We tried to piece the night together.

'I can't believe we fucked on someone's lawn,' I said. 'And then the road.'

'We did *what?*'

Oh, God. She doesn't remember. She doesn't remember any of it. Sad, but understandable.

'We had sex at the end of the street,' I said. 'You don't remember?'

'No…I don't remember any of it. I wish I did.'

'Do you remember crying outside of the bar?'

'I was crying? What a drama queen.'

'It was sweet.'

Then the door opened behind us.

'I didn't know you two were up already.'

Samantha squeezed my knee and got up.

'I'll be right back,' she whispered.

'Okay. I'll be here.'

I pulled my hat even lower over my eyes and hugged myself. I was tired but I was smiling.

There's no fucking way that this is going to work, I thought. *I have to go now. Fuck.*

I heard some rough sounds coming from inside the house. I shriveled up into my shell.

'I'm *not* driving to the Cape by myself, Samantha.'

'But we have maps.'

'I'm NOT driving to the Cape by myself, Samantha.'

'But…'

Son of a bitch.

I pushed myself off the stoop. The grating sound of reality clanged like a rusty cowbell around my neck. Samantha came out. Her eyes were low now too, defeated. She sat next to me.

'Fuck. Damn woman,' she said.

Then Sissy came to the doorway. I shook my head and held up my hands.

'I don't want to screw you up,' I said. 'I've got to go anyway. I have work tomorrow. I don't want to screw you up.'

'No no no,' said Sissy. 'You're not screwing us up.'

She paused. She was thinking.

This could be good.

Samantha and I clasped hands.

Sex all day sex all day. Still a chance. Maybe.

Sissy spoke kindly. 'We don't have to go to the Cape today, Samantha. We can go tomorrow. That way we can sleep here tonight and we can leave really early tomorrow and I can do some cleaning around the house.'

Wow. This wasn't what we were shooting for but this was good. Samantha was grinning a big shit eating grin.

'Okay, Mom.'

I knitted my brows together, trying to look helpless. I *was* helpless. This was out of my hands. *Didn't I have a plan once? Ages ago.*

Sissy disappeared into the echoes of the house. The door closed. Samantha, freshly animated and optimistic, turned to me and said, 'Now we have to get her out of the house for a while so we can have sex.'

'In every room?'

'In every room.'

'How do we do that?'

'I don't know. But this is good.'

And it was good.

We decided to explore our crime scene from the night before. We put on shoes and grabbed a couple of cigarettes.

As we moved down the street, I couldn't help but feel guilty, but excitedly so. Like two animals, we'd left our stinky mark up and down this motherfucker. I kept looking over my shoulder.

As we neared the crime scene we started pointing and laughing. The lawn had been trampled. It looked like two bears had slept there the night before. The short bank that pushed out to the edge of the road was clawed up and dug up and tore up and dirt and leaves covered the pavement in a pattern that strangely resembled the outline of a man and a woman. Fucking.

'Do you remember?' I asked.

'Oh, my god.'

'Do you remember?'

Please remember at least some of it. It's in that pretty head, I know it. But…no.

'Oh my god,' she said. Then, 'What's that?'

'What's what?'

Something was lying in the grass. We knew what it was but we didn't know what it was. Samantha slowed and I tap danced over to it. I looked around and snatched it up. Pink panties. I quickly stuffed them into my back pocket.

'Your fucking panties,' I said.

'Oh, my god.'

We hustled back up the street before we were recognized. The faces of sleepy, puffy eyed strangers pressed up against windows as we skirted past.

***

Samantha was naked in a bathtub, sitting in a few inches of warm water. My hand was pressed flat against her back. I'd just washed my face and my hands and brushed my teeth. From a small cup, she poured water over her head. I was next to the tub, on my knees. The water in the tub was low, but I was overflowing. I dropped my head onto my arm.

'I really do love you,' I whispered.

Then I wanted to cry. But I didn't.

'Are you okay?' she asked.

I nodded.

'Yeah...I'm okay,' I said.

I picked up my head and looked at Samantha. She was sitting in the tub, naked, all wet, and she looked so innocent, so pretty, so...fucking trusting. I was moved, completely. My eyes were sad and she recognized my sadness and we kissed. I felt better then. Samantha made me feel better.

***

'So, David, why are you writing all of this? Why are you writing all of this and sending it 3000 miles to my daughter?'

Sissy was talking to me. I was staring at a plate of pancakes and eggs and a glass of chocolate milk. We were inside a warm diner just down the street from Ledgewood and my stomach was queasy and my eyes were so tired. Sissy was across from me and Samantha was sitting next to me. I'd eaten about a third of my breakfast and that was all I was going to eat. My focus had shifted to keeping myself in the chair and off of the floor. But Sissy was talking to me.

'David?'

'Yeah? Oh, yeah. Why am I writing this? I'm…'

I sucked on my bottom lip and sat up straight and rubbed my hands together. Samantha turned to get a better look at me. She wanted to hear this too. And rightfully so. She was one of the stars of this tale. I smiled nervously. Then I began.

'Well, for starters, let me just say that I'm very grateful and thankful that I got to meet you this week, Sissy. You didn't know me, fuck, *Samantha* didn't know me, and you let me into your family, your…*life*. I thank you for that.'

Sissy nodded and took a bite of sausage.

Samantha rubbed my leg, encouragingly. I continued.

'When I was out in Seattle a few months ago, I was on another planet. Just like now. And I...I didn't know that I would meet Samantha then. God knows I was looking for her. And...*creepily*, maybe, *freakishly*, kinda, I found her, we found each other.'

Samantha took my hand. It calmed me.

'And I didn't want to let that go then. I didn't want it to disappear. God knows it could have. And so we made the effort. And now, this week, this...means so much to me I don't know why. Wait...Yes, I do.'

Sissy was watching me but not austerely. Her blue eyes were soft and kind. Samantha was smiling. I noticed a speck of egg on her chin. I gingerly, lovingly, wiped it away with my napkin. I drew my attention back to the words.

'Sissy, I'm in love with your daughter. And I think she's in love with me. It's crazy, it's fucked up, we're both *obvious* maniacs, we have our own lives to live 3000 miles apart but...it's real. I can feel that it's real. And for now, I think that can be enough.'

Sissy sighed. She raised her eyebrows.

'So, *why* are you writing this?' she asked.

I answered without thinking.

'Because I have to. I have to write this. I don't ever want to forget it.'

I was suddenly blindsided. Samantha knocked me out of my chair but I stayed on my feet and she was ripping at my clothes.

'Kiss me, you fuck,' she said.

'What?'

She pushed her mouth onto mine and we threw our clothes everywhere and Sissy sat back and smiled. We fell on top of the table. Glasses broke, silverware flew in all directions. The other patrons sat quietly and ate their breakfasts. No one outside of our table could see us. We were in a parallel universe.

Samantha's ass was pressed in my half eaten pancakes. She threw water on my face and then licked it off. Sissy covered her mouth and giggled. Then the table started shaking and we were fucking on our breakfast and our heads were close and we were breathy and hot and the words were coming effortlessly, sensually.

'I love you.'

'I love you.'

'I love you.'

'I love you.'

Sissy read a menu to give us some privacy.

***

Back at the house on Ledgewood, Samantha and I sat on the mossy lawn in the sun. Samantha was on my lap. I held her.

'You're strong,' she said.

I'm not that strong, I thought. *It's all an illusion. I'm a walking disaster, my life a cautionary tale for the better adjusted.*

But I smiled anyway. Then I pulled a piece of grass and chewed on it.

***

We were curled up on a red sofa in the studio. We were in our monster suit. Arms, legs, penis, vagina. Two heads. Samantha's mother was going to run some errands but not before snapping a picture of the beast that was us. She took the picture. We giggled. Then she left. We were alone. We didn't know what to do with ourselves. Samantha ran upstairs. I told her I'd be there in a minute.

I called my mother and told her I'd be coming back tonight. She understood. Mothers always understand. I hung up and plugged in my cell phone. Then I went to the bathroom and then I went upstairs.

Samantha was curled up on a twin bed. She was so sleepy. I climbed up next to her. The room was very bright and hot. We lay close.

'Hey.'

'Hey.'

We kissed, we cuddled and we touched. We were slow, deliberate. We were miles away from fucking in every room of the house but that was okay. The bed was small and we were wrapped up in each other and we fell asleep. I was still there. She was still there. I was so glad she talked me into staying. I was so glad she didn't go to the Cape. We slept. We were so tired. We slept. And that was enough.

***

It was late afternoon, early evening. We were driving. Samantha sat next to me. The sun was slinking down in the west but I still had to use my visor from time to time. I'd forgotten my sunglasses.

'Where is the movie theatre?' I asked.

'It's off of Moon Street in Hudson. I think we missed it.'

'I didn't even *see* anything.'

'Me neither.'

I was touching Samantha's leg. She was touching

my hand. We held hands. We were slow. Everything was okay. But the cowbell of reality still clanged around my neck, and Samantha's too, only it was no longer in the form of her mother's stern voice from the morning, but of something much more visceral, heavy, something *now*. It was in the car with us, it was in the music, it was in our hands as we touched, it was in the lights that we moved through, it was in the road, it was in the sun…The sun was in my eyes. I dropped the visor and sighed. I was getting heavy…and sad.

'I don't think we're going to find it,' I said.

'Yeah.'

Then I had a bad idea.

'Do you want to go to my hometown? It's not that far away.'

Samantha slid up in her seat. She crossed her legs and sat in the lotus position.

'Yeah?' she asked.

'Yeah. We're right here at the Mass Pike. This is the way I go home. We could get on right now. We could be there in no time, we could see a movie—'

'And I could meet your mom and your dad and your dog and your cat?'

I cringed. *Fuck*. I recognized my bad idea. I wasn't ready for that yet. Samantha didn't understand my discomfort.

'Ugh…ah, no…I'd just zip through town and we could see a movie and get some dinner. And then I'd bring you back.'

'But…why?'

My parents are crazy which is why I'm crazy. Our house is old, older than your uncle's house. My father is a cross between Jack Nicholson and John Cougar but he's never been in any movies and he doesn't write songs. My mother is small and kind and has a fondness for yard sales. We're a disaster. My whole family is a…wonderful disaster. But it's not all bad…It's not bad at all, really, but…I'm not ready for that yet. This week has gone so well, I don't want to scare you away. And believe me, it would. You have to know me for years to get me…but you seem to get me already. That's amazing. But..no…no, I have to be ready for that.

'I'm wigging out, Samantha,' I said. 'I have to be ready…I'm not ready today.'

And things finally came full circle: *I* was the chicken shit and Samantha was the bat shit. We made it to Washburn before I fully understood this concept. We got off the exit and turned around, the sun now at our backs and out of my eyes.

***

We were quiet. I was quietly flipping out. I didn't know what I was doing anymore. Samantha offered me a cigarette.

'Thank you,' I said. 'I'm sorry…I'm out of it.'

'It's okay. We can go back to Hudson and get Mexican.'

Finally, a good idea. I love it.

'That's a good idea, Samantha.'

'I know.'

We drove down route 10, heading east. We talked. We were calm. We were married. We'd known each other only a few days.

'Tell me your scariest story,' said Samantha.

We talked and we talked and we shared. It all came very easy. I drove slowly. I listened to her. She listened to me. The sun was going down. The sky was pink and purple and blue.

Back in Hudson, I found a place to park just off of Moon Street. We got out and it was twilight and the town was colorful. We walked hand in hand to a Mexican restaurant.

Inside, we were greeted by a big fake lizard that said something in Spanish. We smiled at each other and then a hostess with a heavy southern accent brought us to a patio out back. It was nice, but we'd soon regret it. The mosquitoes were horrible.

My hat was low. We'd been telling dirty stories. A waiter took our order and then left.

'So...I can't believe you were trying to get me to come over that night,' said Samantha.

'I was.'

'Did you wave to me?'

I thought about it. Then I grinned and said, 'In a way, I suppose.'

We laughed. Samantha sipped on a Mexican beer. I sipped on my soda. Our food came. I wanted to throw rice and beans at Samantha. I didn't tell her this. Or maybe I did. We ate. We talked. We laughed. We got bitten by mosquitoes. They attacked Samantha more than me. I felt bad about that. We settled up the bill and I was suddenly very poor. We left. As we moved out, the big fake lizard popped up and whispered, 'Adios, my little lovers.'

We blushed and pressed into each other. The cowbells around our necks clanged loudly.

***

At a stoplight.

'Look at that shit,' I said, pointing.

'What?'

'Look.'

Across the street from us was a big neon sign
that read, 'Cinema.'

'We're fucking idiots,' I said.

'Yes we are.'

We held hands. Bonnie 'Prince' Billy sang sad
songs for us as we drove toward Main Street. Then
Chess. Then Ledgewood. It was dark out. It was
eight o'clock. I had to leave.

***

'Goodbye, Sissy. Thank you for everything.'

'Goodbye, David.'

We embraced. And it was right, good. Despite
her weird flirtations, she had been my mother too
these last few days.

'You'll come to see us soon?' she asked.

'Yes, very soon.'

'Good. Samantha will be happy.'

I'll be happy too.

Samantha stood in the doorway.

'Let's go outside, David,' she said.

'Okay.'

We were calm but hyperaware. We didn't want to
miss a fucking thing. Sissy pressed a large yellow
bag into my palm.

'Don't forget this,' she said with a smile.

I smiled back.

'Of course not.'

The bag was filled with M&Ms. She hoped that by ridding the house of candy she might somehow deter future spills.

You never know.

I waved a last time to Sissy and followed Samantha outside into the night. I put the yellow bag into the back of my truck. Then I gave Samantha everything that I could give her.

'Take my fleece. Take my basketball. Take my love. Take my madness. Take my eyes.'

I popped an eye out and offered it to her. She pressed her lips together and shook her head.

'You can keep your eyes, David. You'll need them.'

'You're probably right.'

'I'm always right.'

'C'mere.'

And we rushed into each other's arms, and it was tight, and strong, and warm, and it was the last time we'd get to be the monster suit for a while. And so we lingered. We lingered in each other's arms.

'I wish I could give you more,' she said.

'You've given me plenty, Samantha. We've got time.'

We parted but we were still connected. Samantha looked at me with those hazel eyes.

'We've got time?' she asked.

'Yes.'

We kissed. We kissed. And we were slow, and sad, and happy. We parted. I got into my truck. She backpedaled to the bottom of the steps. I waved. She waved. We'd done this before but this time it was different. This time I wasn't coming back in a few days.

'I'll call you in two hours,' I said.

'Call me in two hours.'

'I will.'

'I know you will.'

I love you.

I love you.

I love you.

I love you.

I started the truck and drove away. Samantha slunk sadly up the cement steps and into the house. I turned onto Chess. Samantha's mother stopped her in the hallway. I called my mother to let her know I was on my way home.

['Samantha?' asked Sissy.]

'Hey, Mom. It's me. I'm on my way home.'

['Yes, Mom?']

How was everything?' she asked.

['Why was your shirt tucked into David's pocket last night?']

I sighed.

[Samantha sighed.]

'Everything was great, Mom. I'm nutty nuts for this girl.'

['Mom, just let it go. Can't you see I'm fucking fruitcake for this guy?']

My mother nodded. I could hear her nod through the phone. Mothers understand.

[Samantha's mother nodded. Her face was kind. Mothers understand.]

Acknowledgments

Thanks to my family and friends for all and everything. Thanks to Pablo D'Stair for being my white knight. And thanks to you, dear reader. Thanks to you.

Mel Bosworth is the author of *Freight* (Folded Word Press, 2011) and *When the Cats Razzed the Chickens* (Folded Word Press, 2009). Mel lives, breathes, and laughs in western Massachusetts.

Visit him at eddiesocko.blogspot.com.